CENTURION

CENTURION

Jamie Word

Columbus, Ohio

This book is a work of fiction. The names, characters and events in this book are the products of the author's imagination or are used fictitiously. Any similarity to real persons living or dead is coincidental and not intended by the author.

The views and opinions expressed in this book are solely those of the author and do not reflect the views or opinions of Gatekeeper Press. Gatekeeper Press is not to be held responsible for and expressly disclaims responsibility of the content herein.

Centurion

Published by Gatekeeper Press
2167 Stringtown Rd, Suite 109
Columbus, OH 43123-2989
www.GatekeeperPress.com

Copyright © 2022 by Jamie Word
All rights reserved. Neither this book, nor any parts within it may be sold or reproduced in any form or by any electronic or mechanical means, including information storage and retrieval systems, without permission in writing from the author. The only exception is by a reviewer, who may quote short excerpts in a review.

ISBN (paperback): 9781662920974

Contents

Chapter 1 1
Chapter 2 6
Chapter 3 10
Chapter 4 15
Chapter 5 19
Chapter 6 24
Chapter 7 29
Chapter 8 33
Chapter 9 37
Chapter 10 42
Chapter 11 49
Chapter 12 53
Chapter 13 59
Chapter 14 62
Chapter 15 68
Chapter 16 75
Chapter 17 80
Chapter 18 83

Chapter 1

Covenant City, Nevada

Firefighters were battling a blaze at an apartment complex. The police were keeping spectators back out of the way from the firefighters' work. Paramedics were on the scene, tending to people who'd been rescued from the burning building. The media was there covering the story for their respective organizations.

Suddenly, a red, white, and blue blur streaked over the assembly, heading toward the burning building. Stopping on the first floor of the burning building was a costumed man with a cape. He had a full beard and auburn hair. His costume consisted of a white bodysuit with no sleeves for his arms and a blue star on his chest, red wrist bands, red boots, and a yellow belt, a long red cape completing the attire.

The caped man scanned the building with his super vision, seeing an elderly man trapped by the flames on the third floor. With a burst of super speed, he raced up the stairs to the third floor, making eye contact with the trapped man. The trapped man looked at him with an incredulous expression on his face.

"Don't worry, sir," the hero said to the man, calming him a bit. "I'll have you out of here in a moment. Just relax."

"Help me, please!" the man pleaded.

The hero walked through the flames unharmed and wrapped an arm around the elderly man, saying, "I've got you. Now, let's get you out of here."

The hero inhaled deeply and then exhaled a gust of super breath into the flames barring their path, extinguishing the fire. The hero then flew the elderly man out of the burning building and delivered him safely to the paramedics outside.

"Look after him," the hero instructed the paramedics. "I'm needed elsewhere."

Elsewhere over the city, an airplane was struggling to remain aloft. Smoke was billowing from one of the engines as the plane began descending toward the streets below, far from the airport. People below the descending plane began screaming in panic as they saw the end approaching. The pilot and his copilot struggled in vain to try to pull the nose of the plane up, and the passengers were in a panic as well.

Suddenly, a red, white, and blue streak closed on the plane. The hero who had rescued the man from the apartment complex fire mere moments before was underneath the plane. He exhaled a gust of super breath to put out the fire from the smoking engine, and then he supported the descending plane on his shoulders. With an exertion of super strength, he raised the nose of the plane and guided it to the airport. He landed the plane safely on the runway and then flew away, waving to the cheering crowd below.

He flew back to the apartment complex that had been on fire, landing in the midst of the emergency personnel to check on things. The fire department had put out the fire by that time. A young woman with dark hair and a press pass approached him. Accompanying her was a blond-haired man with a camera. The hero noted their arrival with curiosity.

"Excuse me. Claire Jackson of the *Covenant City Crier*," the woman identified herself. "Who are you?"

"I'm an Ardorian Centurion," the hero answered.

"Centurion, huh?" Claire responded with a smile. "So, Centurion, why haven't we seen you on the scene before?"

"It took me a little over a week to get acclimated to my new home," Centurion replied. "Is everyone all right here?"

"Thanks to you," Claire reported. "By the way, this is my photographer, Dave Pierce."

"Nice to meet you, Dave," Centurion greeted the starry-eyed young man.

"Wow! A real superhero here in Covenant City!" Dave sighed in awe.

"What's your story?" Claire asked Centurion.

"I'm here to help. I'm a friend," Centurion answered.

"Where are you from? Tell me your story," Claire implored him.

"I'm from the planet Ardoria," Centurion answered. "My home world was destroyed, and I'm afraid I may be the sole survivor."

"So, you're an alien from another planet?" Claire inquired.

"Yes, I am," Centurion admitted. "It took me over a week to learn about this planet's history and cultures. Today marks my first outing in public."

"Well, we're thankful for your intervention on our behalf," Claire said in appreciation. "What brought you to Earth?"

"My ship was damaged, and I got to your moon before it finally died on me," Centurion explained. "I was able to determine that this was a life-sustaining planet, that there was life here. I flew from your moon to Earth without my spaceship."

"You flew through open space from the moon to Earth without any form of life support or protection?" Claire asked incredulously.

"We Ardorians don't need to breathe, and we're impervious to the rigors of space," Centurion responded. "We use the spaceships because they're faster."

"This story is getting juicy," Claire remarked as she jotted down notes. "How do you spell Ardoria?"

"A-r-d-o-r-i-a," Centurion spelled it out for her.

"So, are you born with these powers of yours?" Claire asked.

"We are born with our abilities," Centurion answered. "We spend our childhood learning to control our abilities fully, and then we choose occupations."

"And what was your occupation?" Claire inquired.

"I was a soldier," Centurion replied. "I joined the Ardorian Centurions when I was eighteen, over twenty years ago."

"What about family? Do you have a family?" Claire asked.

"I had a wife, Ilyana, and two children—a son, Cor, and a daughter, Adara," Centurion informed her solemnly. "As far as I know, they were on Ardoria when it exploded."

"I'm so sorry," Claire gasped sympathetically.

"If you'll excuse me, I should go," Centurion suggested.

"Will we see you again?" Claire inquired.

"Probably so," Centurion declared with a slight smile.

Centurion took flight, departing the scene and ascending high into the sky.

Claire turned to Dave and said, "We've got the scoop of the century!"

Chapter 2

It was later that same day in the bustling Covenant City. On the streets, there was a police chase in progress. A souped-up sports car was speeding along, driving a bit recklessly. The police cruisers were having a hard time keeping up, falling behind more and more as the chase wore on. A *Covenant City Crier* news copter was also in pursuit, Claire Jackson and Dave Pierce in the copter. Claire was speaking into her digital recorder while Dave was taking pictures of the chase scene with his camera.

"It looks like the Camaro has been souped up because it's exceeding the maximum speed of the police cars," Claire said into her recorder. "Apparently, these maniacs in the sports car cut off a school bus and ran it off the road before racing away from the scene. Nobody knows what their deal is, and it doesn't look like anybody's gonna find out, either. They're gonna kill somebody, possibly even themselves!"

It was at that time that a familiar red, white, and blue blur sped past the news copter, closing on the police chase. The blur zipped over the police cars like they weren't even moving and quickly closed on the speeding Camaro. Centurion swooped in front and put his boot on the front of the car, slowing his flight and thereby slowing the car. Immediately, the cackling punks in the car extended handguns out of the windows and began firing shots at the hero. Responding to that threat, Centurion's eyes began glowing red. Then, twin red beams shot out from his eyes as he targeted each punk's gun in turn, heating the guns until the punks yelped and dropped their weapons.

Seconds later, Centurion had stopped the car as the police circled the Camaro and stepped out of their cruisers, guns drawn. The police quickly took the disarmed punks into custody, a group of long-haired, hippie-like guys who were giggling and cackling maniacally, clearly on something. Centurion stood in front of the car as a cop approached him, the news copter landing not far away.

"You're Centurion, right?" the cop inquired as Claire and Dave emerged from the news copter and raced toward Centurion.

"I suppose I am," Centurion replied politely, a gentle smile upon his face. "I guess that's what everybody's calling me now."

"Thank you for stopping these guys," the cop declared in appreciation. "Their car was just too fast for us, and obviously whatever they're on has them too impaired to operate a motor vehicle. Fortunately, no one was injured on the school bus they ran off the road."

"That's a good thing," Centurion remarked as Claire and Dave reached him.

"Claire Jackson of the *Covenant City Crier*," Claire introduced herself to Centurion jovially. "Do you think we can get another interview now?"

Suddenly, a massive, unending roar caught his attention, and he looked back over his shoulder to see a rather large tornado closing on the city from out in the desert. Claire and Dave were surprised as well, and Dave began taking photographs.

"Find shelter," Centurion advised them. "I'll try to stop it."

Centurion took flight, racing toward the large twister.

"To the chopper, Dave!" Claire exclaimed as she began running toward the news copter, prompting Dave to follow her.

"What?" Dave responded incredulously. "Are you crazy?"

"It's a story, Dave! Come on!" Claire scolded him as they got into the news copter. "Pilot, get us as close to that tornado as you can! Dave, keep snapping pictures!"

As the *Covenant City Crier* news copter lifted off and headed toward the tornado, Centurion hovered in midair as if to contemplate the situation.

"I've never dealt with anything like this before," Centurion muttered to himself as he studied the tornado. "The winds are rotating in a counterclockwise direction at great speed, and the entire thing is moving toward the city at an alarming rate. The damage that thing will do to this city will be catastrophic, as will the loss of life if I don't stop it."

Then, another sound got his attention, the sound of a helicopter in flight. Looking in that direction, he saw the *Covenant City Crier* helicopter flying toward the tornado. He shook his head in disbelief at the spectacle of them moving toward the tornado. Without a moment to lose, he flew into the tornado as they watched him. He began circling the tornado in the opposite direction of its rotation, flying faster and faster in a circle. Within moments, he'd unraveled the tornado, and it dissipated. Centurion flew over to the news copter, hovering nearby.

"Well, I guess that takes care of that," Claire muttered, as if disappointed.

"What do you think you're doing?" Centurion rebuked them. "It was very dangerous of you to try to get a closer look at the tornado. You could've been knocked from the sky by debris and killed."

"It was a story for the few brief moments it was there," Claire reminded him. "It's a story, and I'm a reporter, hence the chase."

"You're a story chaser, not a storm chaser," Centurion advised her. "Storm chasing is best left to the professionals. You don't know enough about it to try it on for size like this."

"Relax," Claire replied. "The danger's past now, and I have a story to go to press with. You saved the day again."

"Just be more careful next time," Centurion suggested.

"How about that interview now?" Claire asked.

"I think you've already got your story for the day, Ms. Jackson," Centurion chuckled. "I'll see you around."

Centurion flew away from them.

"Let's get back to the *Crier* and get this story to the presses," Claire said to Dave with an eager smile on her face.

"Okay," Dave replied, a relieved look on his face.

Chapter 3

Two days later

A private plane was streaking through the skies. Sitting on the plane, reading a copy of the *Covenant City Crier*, was a well-dressed man, bald, with a goatee. Seated on the plane around him in various seats were red-colored robots with white sensors. Seated next to the man was a young woman in a business suit, looking over an itinerary in her hands. The bald man with the newspaper looked disappointed.

"This is absolutely unbelievable," the bald man with the goatee muttered in dismay. "My visit relegated to page two of my hometown paper, while this alien freak who only made his appearance two days ago gets front-page coverage. It's absurd. I am Senator Alexander Atlas, Covenant City's favorite son. My brainchild, Atlascorp, employs most of the city's residents in one capacity or another. My Atlas Foundation makes charitable donations to several causes in the community. My work as a United States Senator helps to bring jobs and opportunities to the city. I am on the verge of a potential run for the White House, for goodness' sake, but do I get front-page coverage in my hometown paper? No. They plaster this visitor from the stars on the front page.

"Look at him, a proverbial messianic figure for the masses to worship like blind sheep. For crying out loud, he's from another planet altogether, and he's a soldier from another planet at that. He rescued a tenant at an apartment complex fire while the firefighters battled the blaze. He rescued a plane from crashing into the city and stopped it from potentially killing many people. He stopped a carload of doped-up hooligans in a souped-up sports car from terrorizing the city. After that, he stopped an EF-4 tornado from devastating the city, performing yet another miracle in the process.

"They fawn all over this freak like he's a god come down from the heavens to bring salvation to them. Why, I'll bet they even drool over him. This upcoming press conference was meant to be a starting point for my march to the White House. Now, it's a platform to reclaim my rightful place at the top of the pecking order from this extraterrestrial nuisance. He makes me sick."

"Well, sir, you can make this press conference both options at once," the woman sitting beside him suggested. "You can start your momentum for a run at the presidency and recapture the public eye from this Centurion character too."

"In the last two days, he has been the big story for the media all over the country, not just in my hometown," Senator Atlas grumbled. "Every television news program pushes the attention onto this alien freak. He's on the front page of every newspaper in the country. You can't tune in to a radio talk show without being bombarded by the story of this superpowered menace to the security of this planet.

"Eventually, all that hoopla will play out," the woman sought to assure him.

"I'm hoping to expunge the need for eventually," Senator Atlas remarked. "Before I stand at the podium for that press conference, I intend to check in with Dr. Cross at Atlascorp. I'm hoping he has made some progress with the projects he's been working on. I can't wait to see what he has for me."

"I'll have everything ready for you at the press conference, sir," the woman stated.

"I'm sure you will, Ms. Watson," Senator Atlas replied in an appreciative tone. "With my security bots around me, I'll have nothing to fear. I must remember to thank Dr. Cross once again for the magnificent work on my security bots."

"They are quite formidable," Ms. Watson remarked. "Not only do they save the taxpayers money by not having to provide your security, but they are far more durable and capable than traditional bodyguards."

"They're top-of-the-line all right," Senator Atlas declared. "Built-in blasters, superhuman strength, and armor plating make them impressive bodyguards. Built at Atlascorp to be my personal security, they are the best that money can buy. Others on Capitol Hill are strongly considering investing in a few security bots for their personal entourage. I've heard even the president has shown interest as well."

Senator Atlas glanced back at the newspaper in his hand.

"Page two! I should be page one. Instead, I play second fiddle to a superpowered alien from another planet. It's not only a travesty; it's a slight against me by this reporter Claire Jackson. Her front-page article on Centurion reeks of hero worship, while the article on me seems uninspired," Senator Atlas lamented.

Senator Atlas retrieved his cell phone and pressed a button, making a call.

"Hello, Senator Atlas. It's a pleasure to hear from you. How are you?" came a male voice on the other end of the phone call.

"A bit annoyed, Dr. Cross," Senator Atlas responded quite frankly. "Have you seen the latest *Crier*?"

"A travesty, sir," Dr. Cross answered. "Your return should've been front page."

"Indeed," Senator Atlas responded. "How are things at Atlascorp?"

"All goes well," Dr. Cross replied proudly.

"I'll be arriving in Covenant City soon, and I'm expecting a full briefing upon my arrival. I want progress reports on all outstanding projects, and I want analysis reports on this Centurion character," Senator Atlas informed Dr. Cross.

"As you wish, sir," Dr. Cross replied.

"Prepare for the briefing," Senator Atlas instructed. "I'll be there soon."

"Yes, sir," Dr. Cross responded obediently. "Welcome home, sir."

"Thank you," Senator Atlas replied with a slight smile. "Goodbye."

"Goodbye, sir," Dr. Cross said as they concluded their phone conversation.

"Days of hero worship and he still warrants front-page coverage in *my* hometown newspaper," Senator Atlas grumbled under his breath as he looked at the photograph of Centurion on the front page. "Like a Greek god in spandex, come down from the heavens to protect us all from harm and save us from our baser selves. Gifted with unfathomable physical powers. Blessed with powers that required no work. My own physical abilities were built up by hard work and determination on my part. *I* am the one who put Covenant City on the map with my political and business successes. *I* am the one who got government contracts for my city. *I* am the one who built Atlascorp from the ground up. It should be *me* that they cheer and admire... that they adore."

"Without you, they'd be nothing... less than nothing," Ms. Watson added. "Most of them work for you because of Atlascorp and are able to feed their families. They owe you everything, and they should never have forgotten that."

"Ms. Watson, sometimes I don't know if you're stroking my ego or being condescending," Senator Atlas commented in a half-annoyed state before turning his attention to the cockpit. "Mr. Williams. ETA?"

"Ten minutes," the pilot of the plane informed him.

"Excellent," Senator Atlas responded contentedly. "That'll give me just enough time for a workout before my briefing with Dr. Cross."

Chapter 4

Washington, DC

An old, grizzled general sat at a conference table with a few men in suits. A lit cigar was in his mouth as he eyed the suited men warily. The men in suits had file folders on the table in front of them, and there was also a file folder on the table in front of the general.

"General Jeremiah Hawkins, you have been tasked with the assessment of the potential threat of this Centurion character," one of the suited men said to the cigar-smoking general in their midst. "We want to know if he poses any threat to this country... or this world. For all we know, he may be the advance scout for an alien invasion of Earth. If he is a threat to us, you are authorized to recommend action against him. Do you understand this?"

"Son, I may be old, but I'm not stupid," General Hawkins responded, as if annoyed by a thinly veiled insinuation. "I will investigate this visitor from the stars and will inform you of my findings, as well as my recommendation of action.

"For those of you who are ignorant of my credentials, I am a Vietnam veteran, and I've served in the United States Army for over half a century. I rose through the ranks of service to the rank of general, receiving a plethora of commendations along the way. I have served my country in peace time and in times of war for longer than most of you have been alive. I've commanded small squads of soldiers and whole platoons from command posts. I have worked closely with the Pentagon and both the legislative and executive branches of this United States government in both war time and peace time.

"I've seen men die on the battlefield, many good friends. I've seen the evils of humanity up close and personal, the depravity of human villainy, the basest of human nature. Some of you are rather green when it comes to understanding evil. You naively think our enemies will act honorably, but you're wrong. Evil men do not follow a code of honor; they follow the desires of their hearts by any means necessary. In order to combat evil, you must first understand it.

"I have led soldiers to victory both on the battlefield and from remote command posts. I have faced death and evil, and I have prevailed through knowledge and strategy. I've seen the worst of humanity and the best of humanity, both in the same place. I've seen our enemies send women to deliver booby-trapped babies in attempts to kill us. I've seen fanatical psychopaths slaughter their own people in the pursuit of power. In Vietnam, the barber who shaved you in the morning could be the same person who tried to slit your throat that night. Supposedly innocent civilians in villages turned out to be cold-blooded assassins, what we commonly call terrorists in the present-day vernacular.

"I can assess this situation with the same precision and clarity as I assessed threats to our soldiers on the field of battle over the years. I will view this stranger from the stars with an objective eye, hoping for the best while contemplating the alternative. Of course, I'm certain this is why you've chosen me for this assignment. I will discern this alien's intent, and if it is within my power, should he be a threat, find a way to neutralize him. This I promise you on my honor as a member of the United States military charged with the protection of the American people."

"On the table in front of you is everything we have at this point on Centurion in that file folder," one of the suited men informed him. "Study it well and add this knowledge to your own. Use it to gauge your investigation and weigh your options. As they say, knowledge is power, and we hope this empowers you."

"Knowledge is power, and I'm sure this will prove useful to me," General Hawkins replied. "I will study this file on my way to Covenant City. I will interview Claire Jackson of the *Covenant City Crier* to see what insights I can take from her. Also, I'll interview as many people as I can, people who may have had contact with the alien. Eventually, I intend to meet the man himself and speak with him personally."

"You won't be going alone," one of the suited men said. "A battalion of soldiers will accompany you to Covenant City to provide security for you and to assist you in facilitating your mission. You will be provided a computer with a secure direct link to us, so you can transmit all data you find to us in regular communications."

"I will provide regular updates for you until I have fully assessed the situation," General Hawkins vowed. "I suppose I will be leaving immediately."

"You will," one of the suited men answered. "Godspeed, General."

"Thank you," General Hawkins responded as he stood up and collected the file folder from the table in preparation for leaving the room.

Chapter 5

Covenant City, Nevada

In the *Covenant Crier* building, Claire Jackson was at her desk, proofreading her latest story on her computer. Dave Pierce walked over to her desk, his camera in hand.

"Hey, Claire. What's up?" Dave greeted her.

"Oh, hi, Dave. I'm just proofreading my story before I submit it to the editor," Claire responded politely.

"Another Centurion story, huh?" Dave surmised.

"He is what makes the news world go round nowadays," Claire remarked. "Ever since his debut two days ago, the world just can't get enough of this guy, and I'm feeling the same way about it. I mean, he's so powerful, yet he's devoted to doing good for others. He seemed genuinely concerned for us after that tornado as well."

"I was genuinely concerned for us too," Dave chimed in.

"Oh, knock it off, Dave. I wasn't gonna get us killed," Claire assured him. "We were just moving closer to get a better scoop; that's all. Anyway, he's been a bona fide hero ever since day one. He rescued that plane and landed it safely at the airport.

He rescued that guy that was trapped in that apartment fire just before that. He stopped those doped-up hoodlums in the souped-up sports car, preventing them from killing anybody. He stopped that tornado. Is there anything he can't do?"

"Super strength, super speed, invulnerable skin, the power of flight, and super breath, not to mention the super senses required to detect those emergencies and respond to them in such a timely manner and those wicked eyebeams. I guess that's the biggest question. We don't know the full extent of his powers, just what he's displayed so far. For all we know, he could have dozens of more abilities at his disposal," Dave stated thoughtfully.

"And, despite all those fantastic powers, he's still so down to earth... even if he is an alien from another planet," Claire commented. "I wonder how many of us would be that way if we had such powers. I'd like to think we'd cling to our better selves under such circumstances, but I know some of us don't have better selves to cling to."

"It's sad, too," Dave lamented. "Humankind has untold potential for good, but too many people stray down that path of evil, including, unfortunately, people in power."

"One does come to mind right off the bat—a certain bald, goateed senator from Covenant City," Claire agreed. "I can't believe he made it into public office without some of his skeletons being dug up. He spared no expense to make sure they stayed hidden away in his closet and away from the view of the people. I can't believe he's as clean cut as he presents himself to be. His speeches are downright reeking of ulterior motive and sinister purpose, like subtle hints that he's not what he appears to be."

"Still, he's presumed innocent until proven guilty," Dave reminded her.

"Yeah, I know," Claire replied. "I guess wealth and power can keep you out of trouble one way or another. Still, some people are presumed guilty until proven innocent. We live in an era of double standards. Senator Atlas used his company's reputation, his abundant wealth, and his silver tongue to get elected into the United States Senate, and I'll bet he's got his eyes on the White House too."

"It's completely possible," Dave admitted. "I take it you wouldn't vote for him if he did run for president."

"Not on your life," Claire decreed fervently. "That man is evil to the core. He just manages to hide it really, really well."

"But you trust Centurion after only two days," Dave said.

"We've been up close and personal with our alien flyboy for these two days," Claire explained. "His deeds and his words match up really well, and he comes across as genuine. If he's lying, he's doing a great job of it. He's been very open about his past with us. I believe he's being honest with us."

"So do I," Dave concurred. "With his powers, he doesn't have to pretend to be a good guy. I don't think we could stop him if he was a bad guy, not without massive casualties on our side. It would probably take a nuke to beat him."

"I'm sure glad he's on our side," Claire proclaimed in relief.

"So am I," Dave added.

"There's never been anyone like him on our planet before, not that I know of anyway," Claire commented. "I mean, mythology is rich with superheroes of their age, but those legends are just that, legends. There are no actual historic records that I've ever seen of the ancient gods and heroes of the world's mythologies. No Thor, no Hercules, no Zeus, no Horus, no Osiris, no Odin, none of them. There are just fictional stories telling of their mythological exploits. I've never heard of evidence of a superpowered being on this planet before. That being said, that doesn't mean there haven't been superpowered beings on this planet before now. Maybe all the stories of mythology are based in some truth, for all I know. I could be wrong, but I could be right."

"Wouldn't it be cool if Hercules or Thor showed up to become superheroes next?" Dave rhetorically inquired. "I mean, if they're real, not fictional."

"Yeah, that might be pretty cool," Claire admitted. "Of course, what are the chances that they might come looking to fight with Centurion? Those mythological beings tended to have massive egos in addition to superhuman powers."

"Yeah, now that wouldn't be too cool," Dave acknowledged. "I'd like to think that, if they were real and they came back, they'd become friends with Centurion and be on his side. I'd like to believe they'd be inspired by his heroic nature."

"Well, we could debate this all day, but I'm on a deadline here, and I really need to get this story to the editor's desk soon," Claire decreed emphatically.

"Oh yeah. I'll just leave you to your work," Dave replied as he began walking away. "See you later."

"Later, Dave," Claire responded as she returned to her work.

Chapter 6

Atlascorp

Covenant City, Nevada

Senator Atlas stood in a lab, flanked by his security bots. A well-dressed black man and a middle-aged white man in a white lab coat stood with the bald, goateed senator. They were watching video footage of Centurion in action, performing various feats of superhuman abilities in a host of heroic actions. Senator Atlas regarded the video footage with contempt in his visage, his loathing of Centurion almost palpable.

"As you can see, he possesses superhuman strength, speed, and durability along with the power of flight. Additionally, he can project rays of heat from his eyes and produce a gust of powerful wind from his mouth, yet he doesn't require air to breathe," the scientist informed the senator while they watched the video footage.

"Then his lungs serve no purpose other than to produce wind gusts like that," Senator Atlas discerned. "Very good, Dr. Cross. Any luck locating his base of operations?"

"None so far, sir, but we're still trying," Dr. Cross answered.

"Please do," Senator Atlas implored the scientist.

"He does seem extremely powerful," the black man chimed in. "It would take a lot of strength to support a fully loaded passenger plane like that."

"Yes, Mr. Williams," Senator Atlas concurred. "It appears his accounting of his powers to Claire Jackson of the *Covenant City Crier* was at least somewhat honest. Who knows what other abilities he possesses that he hasn't yet revealed? Have you started on the lead lining for Atlascorp yet, Dr. Cross?"

"The project is underway as we speak," Dr. Cross replied. "It will take considerable time to line all the walls of this facility in lead, however."

"Take whatever time is needed," Senator Atlas instructed him. "Fortunately, for now, he doesn't suspect a thing, but I'd hate for him to start snooping with that penetrating vision of his and see some of the things we're working on here."

"We do know that he heads south once he leaves the city, so it appears his base is somewhere south of here," Dr. Cross informed the senator.

"I'd suspect it would be somewhere he could keep it hidden from prying eyes," Senator Atlas suggested. "Mexico or South America might be a possibility. He could have his base hidden in the South American jungles for all we know. Of course, for all we know, his base could be invisible to the human eye and positioned to avoid inadvertent contact. It might remain hidden for quite some time if that's the case.

"We can't very well send large numbers of personnel into Mexico or South America to search for a hidden base. The authorities there would frown on such a thing, especially if they deemed that it resembled an invasion. Flyovers would likewise be problematic. Such an invasion of their airspace might provoke them into shooting down said aircraft. I could send in robotic emissaries to scout for a hidden base, but that might be met with equal distaste by their governments unless I first open diplomatic channels with them, which could tip Centurion off as to my efforts to locate his base.

"It might be more feasible to have tiny drones tail him back to his headquarters and hope that he doesn't notice them. Of course, with his superhuman senses, it is doubtful that even the quietest drones would escape his notice. For that same reason, it is doubtful we'd be able to attach a tracking device to his clothing and use it to track his movements; his super hearing would hear the ultrasonic signal of the tracking device. Also, we don't know how fast he can fly, so we don't know if a manned aircraft would be able to keep up with him. It would appear that there is no way we can follow him back to his base to locate it.

"As of this moment, we have no agency set up specifically to deal with superhuman beings of great power. We have the military, but what can our soldiers do against the likes of him? I have a few suggestions for my colleagues on Capitol Hill to consider with regards to this matter. Perhaps we can change our situation in due course. I plan on proposing a specialized police force with high-tech equipment to try to deal with superhuman menaces that threaten our society. I also have a proposal for a governing agency for the proposed police force and a proposal for an incarceration facility for those superhuman beings the police force manages to apprehend."

"I suppose Atlascorp will be tapped for the technology," Dr. Cross surmised.

"Actually, I might allow Tech Labs to take on this one," Senator Atlas admitted, much to the surprise of the other two men. "Our labs will be substantially burdened with the projects we already have in the works. Besides, having Tech Labs provide the technological gear and equipment for these projects avoids the appearance of a conflict of interest. They might be second string compared to us, but they'll do admirably. Still, we should develop our own technologies to this end at some point."

"Professor Addington has a rather light load at the moment," Dr. Cross remarked as he gave the idea some thought. "I could put his team to work on the project."

"Make it so," Senator Atlas instructed his chief scientist. "Now, I'm quite interested in what you have been working on for me."

"Well, we almost have the prototype armor online as we speak," Dr. Cross explained. "We're doing some final tests to make sure it's up to par. I'd like it to be in perfect working condition when we present it to you."

"Very good," Senator Atlas responded, pleased with the report.

"It looks a little bulky, but it will increase the wearer's strength and durability immensely. Also, it will have blasters for armaments and thrusters in the boots for jet propulsion flight. We've already got the comm system and the life support system functioning perfectly, and we've got visual enhancement and a tactical combat computer to enhance the wearer's combat prowess," Dr. Cross informed the senator. "It will be quite the formidable battlefield weapon when it's completed. It should be 100 percent complete within a couple of days."

"Excellent," Senator Atlas commended his scientist.

"Who's gonna fly it?" Mr. Williams inquired.

"Whoever I see fit," Senator Atlas answered with a smile. "We might just have the tool to keep Centurion in check... or to take him out."

"It will surpass the capabilities of the security bots," Dr. Cross declared.

"Outstanding," Senator Atlas voiced his great pleasure at the news.

Chapter 7

Covenant City, Nevada

Centurion was flying through the air, and suddenly, a robotic voice sounded in his ear, saying, "You are directly in the path of the meteor, sir."

"Thank you, computer," Centurion replied just before he flew straight up into the sky at super speed, breaking the sound barrier in the process.

Centurion flew out into space to intercept a large meteor approaching the earth. Centurion closed on the meteor quickly, intercepting it a substantial distance from the earth. Centurion began pushing against the meteor, exerting his super strength in an attempt to divert the meteor. Centurion strained in the effort, slowly beginning to shift the meteor's trajectory away from the planet. With the initial success of his effort, his confidence increased, and he pushed harder. He managed to direct its path, steering it past the planet, saving the earth from the potential impact.

Relieved by his success, Centurion smiled at his handiwork. He then flew back toward the earth. With a reduced sense of urgency, he reentered the atmosphere, flying over Covenant City. A moment later, he was flanked by a pair of military jets, one on either side of him. He politely saluted each jet pilot in turn, a friendly smile upon his face. With the danger past, Centurion accelerated, racing from between the two jet fighters and leaving them in the dust. The two pilots were dumbfounded by that feat.

"Outstanding work, sir," the computer declared in Centurion's earpiece comm link.

"Thank you, computer," Centurion responded happily. "I'm sure they'll find out eventually what just happened. So, any luck locating any evidence of any Ardorian survivors other than me?"

"I'm afraid not, sir. If there are any survivors of the planet Ardoria besides you, they are beyond the sensors of any Ardorian remote base," the computer answered.

"So, you linked up with every remote base still operational?" Centurion asked.

"Yes, sir," the computer replied. "There are a number of remote bases that are no longer operational at this time, presumably destroyed. Scans detected no signs of Ardorian survivors in the vicinity of those remaining remote bases."

"Continue scans at regular intervals of six hours," Centurion instructed the computer.

"Yes, sir," the computer stated.

Centurion decreased his flight speed, taking an opportunity to savor the visual as he flew over the ocean. Centurion continued to enjoy the spectacle of nature's wonder as he flew along above the water. He then streaked high up above the clouds, flying just above them and taking in the sight of that beneath him.

"The earth is beautiful," Centurion commented as he marveled at the sight of it. "It reminds me so much of Ardoria in so many ways."

"It is a lush planet with vast resources," the computer declared. "Its diameter is significantly less than Ardoria's was, but it is very much like Ardoria."

"Let's see how long it takes me to circle the earth at top speed," Centurion suggested with an eager grin on his face.

In an instant, Centurion accelerated to full speed. Less than half an hour later, he was back where he started from.

"Time?" Centurion asked.

"Twenty-three minutes and 55.25 seconds," the computer informed him. "An impressive feat, sir."

"Just over twenty minutes," Centurion noted with a smile. "Now I know I can get to anywhere on the planet in about twelve minutes to avert danger to people."

"So, are you returning here or to Covenant City?" the computer inquired.

"Is there anything requiring my attention in Covenant City?" Centurion asked.

"No, sir," the computer informed him.

"Then I'm coming home," Centurion declared.

"Pleasant and safe journey, sir," the computer wished him well.

"I'll take my time this time," Centurion advised the computer. "I'd like to take in the sights a bit more on the way."

"As you wish, sir," the computer said.

Centurion dipped down below the clouds, gazing down upon the earth as he flew along. He felt tranquility as he beheld the wonders of the planet he had taken up residency on. He felt the wind on his face, a gentle sensation despite his speed. He also felt the warmth of the sunshine on his face as he flew along, also a gentle sensation.

Chapter 8

Two days later

Centurion was flying across the United States, and then he felt a little dizzy in the air. He descended to the ground below and landed, kneeling on the ground.

"Are you okay, sir?" the computer inquired.

"I don't know," Centurion confessed, a hand to his head as he knelt on the ground. "I feel a little strange for some unknown reason."

"My instruments detected a strange energy emanating from that meteor you redirected away from the planet two days ago," the computer informed him. "The unusual radiation spread across the entire Earth. It is unknown what effect this has had on the inhabitants of the earth, yourself included. You took a substantially more potent dose of that radiation due to your sustained proximity to the meteor when you diverted it."

"I've never been vulnerable to radiation before," Centurion remarked.

"Perhaps this sort of radiation wasn't typical," the computer surmised. "Perhaps it wasn't radiation as we know it."

"I'm feeling better now," Centurion said as he stood up to his feet again. "I'm not feeling dizzy anymore."

"I'll keep you under observation to see if there are any long-term effects," the computer advised him.

"Of course," Centurion replied as he looked around. "It looks like there's a storm in the distance. I'm seeing a great deal of rotation in the clouds out there."

"You're in an area that is under a tornado warning, sir," the computer declared.

"Well, I think I've found the tornado," Centurion responded as he watched the funnel descend from the cloud to the ground and produce a debris cloud on the ground. "I'm going to put a stop to this before anyone gets hurt."

Centurion flew toward the tornado at high speed. He flew into the twister and began circling it in the opposite direction of its rotation. Before he could unravel the tornado, Centurion began feeling odd again. Moments later, Centurion was being spun around in the vortex, tossed uncontrollably by the tornado. An instant later, he was hurled out of the tornado, his body skipping across the ground. Centurion looked up from the ground to see the tornado tracking back in his direction.

"Sir," the computer tried to warn him.

"I see it," Centurion proclaimed as he started to get to his feet, still a little dizzy.

Debris from the tornado pummeled Centurion before the funnel snatched the hero from the ground and whipped him around in its rotation. Centurion struggled against the dizziness to regain control of his flight, but the tornado continued to spin him around inside it at high speed. After a few moments, Centurion regained control of himself and once again began circling the tornado opposite its rotation. Exerting himself, Centurion managed to unravel that tornado. Upon successfully completing that task, Centurion hovered in midair, looking all around.

"Are you all right, sir?" the computer asked.

"I will be," Centurion vowed. "How's the storm system looking?"

"There's another strong hook echo approximately a mile and a half southeast of you," the computer informed him. "It could possibly form into a tornado."

"I'll be there shortly," Centurion replied.

Centurion began flying off in that direction.

"There are a number of strange cases around the world developing as we speak," the computer revealed. "Some people are experiencing a mild form of radiation poisoning; at least, that's how they're describing it. They're experiencing spells of dizziness, much like yours, only more pronounced. The energy that emanated from the meteor must be somehow affecting them."

"Keep monitoring the situation," Centurion implored the computer. "Let me know how it all plays out. I'm on my way toward the location of the hook echo you detected. I'm feeling all right again, but I don't know how long that will last. I'll see what I can do about this storm system, and then I'm coming home to be checked out."

"I'll keep you abreast of any further developments," the computer assured him.

Chapter 9

Several military helicopters landed at the Covenant City airport. General Hawkins emerged from one of the military helicopters, accompanied by a substantial number of soldiers from all the helicopters. They proceeded to a convoy of military trucks parked at the airport, and they were greeted by a couple of soldiers waiting by the convoy. Those soldiers stood at attention and saluted the general.

"Good afternoon, General Hawkins," one of the soldiers greeted him.

"At ease, men," General Hawkins implored the soldiers as he looked at the trucks. "Is the convoy ready to move out?"

"Ready whenever you are, sir," the soldier replied.

"Good," General Hawkins responded. "I want surveillance established all over this city by evening. Anytime Centurion shows up to save the day, I want surveillance footage to study. I want to know if he has any habits in town, any place he frequents, anybody he has dealings with on a regular basis.

"Lieutenant Wallace, you get your truck to Tech Labs and see what sort of surveillance technology they can offer us. Lieutenant Parker, you get your truck to Atlascorp and see if they can assist us in this endeavor. Somebody get me to the *Covenant City Crier*. I want to talk with that reporter, Ms. Jackson. Everybody else, spread out and start setting up whatever surveillance equipment we already have over as much of the city as possible.

"If Centurion shows himself in Covenant City, I want to know about it. Ultimately, I want to interview Centurion myself. I understand Senator Atlas is back home for a press conference. We should contact him and let him know what's going on so he doesn't get too worried about security. Of course, he's got those robot security guards they built at Atlascorp, so I doubt he's too worried about security these days. Lieutenant Parker, you call Senator Atlas and update him on our presence and what we're doing in his city.

"You've all been briefed, so you all know what to do. I expect to have the surveillance system set up before nightfall, including night-vision surveillance. We've got a lot of work to do, gearing up a city this size, and we don't have a lot of time, so get to it. All right, men, move 'em out! Let's get rolling!"

The soldiers began boarding the trucks, and General Hawkins climbed into the passenger seat of one of the trucks. The trucks began moving out into the city in different directions. The truck transporting General Hawkins made its way to the *Covenant City Crier* building, pulling to a stop in front of the building. General Hawkins and his soldiers disembarked from the truck and marched up the steps of the building, entering through the front door and marching through the offices. The staff of the *Covenant City Crier* observed the soldiers with some concern as they made their way along.

General Hawkins stopped at the desk of Claire Jackson. She was seated at her desk, working on another story. Claire looked up to see the military entourage with General Hawkins, and she was a bit concerned.

"Go tell the editor I'll be interviewing Ms. Jackson," General Hawkins instructed one of his men, making eye contact with Claire and maintaining eye contact with her.

"Yes, sir," one of the soldiers responded, heading off in search of the editor.

"Is something wrong, General Hawkins?" Claire inquired curiously.

"Ms. Jackson, you've had contact with Centurion. After all, you wrote all those stories on him," General Hawkins commented, pulling up a chair to her desk and sitting in that chair with proper posture while removing his hat.

"Yes, I have," Claire admitted.

"I want you to tell me everything you can about him," General Hawkins instructed her. "Anything you can tell me that you didn't print in your articles would be helpful."

"I'm afraid I don't have any other information on him," Claire informed him. "I printed everything I learned from him in those articles."

"Tell me about your conversations with him," General Hawkins insisted. "Can you tell me what he was like? Did he seem nervous, anxious? Was he arrogant?"

"He seemed calm, rational," Claire stated. "He was down to earth, which I know is a little weird to be saying about an alien from another planet. He was patient... except for this one time. He scolded Dave and me for chasing a tornado for our story. He was genuinely concerned for our well-being. He didn't want us risking our lives chasing after a story like that. He seems to be a genuinely good guy."

"Either that or he's a darned good actor," General Hawkins suggested.

"I don't think it was an act," Claire assured him. "I honestly think he was genuine in his concern for us."

"I hope you understand my position in this matter," General Hawkins said. "If he is a threat to us, we need to find out about it as quickly as possible. We need to discover any weaknesses he may have in order to ensure a chance against him if it comes to that. Most of all, we need to find out where he's hiding when he's not flying around this city.

"We have to confront the possibility that he might be an advance scout for an invasion, or he might be the hero he presents himself to be. We must be sure. We can't afford not to know for certain. He is a soldier from another planet, and he is immensely powerful. This should give us pause. What if a thousand more like him show up to conquer our world and make it their own? This is our planet, and we must protect that. Certainly you must understand that."

"I do, but I don't believe he's a threat to our world," Claire declared. "I've been around him a number of times, and he comes across as genuinely good to me. Nothing about him raises any red flags as far as I can tell."

"Well, I appreciate your candor, Ms. Jackson," General Hawkins remarked. "If you can think of anything that might indicate differently, please let us know. We'll be in the city for a while. I think I'd like to talk to your friend Dave now."

"He's probably around here somewhere," Claire replied. "He's one of our photographers, so he waits for me to be sent out on a story and then accompanies me."

"Thank you for your time, Ms. Jackson," General Hawkins declared as he stood up from the chair he was sitting in, placing his hat back on his head.

"You're welcome, General," Claire responded cordially.

Chapter 10

The planet Vetoria

A large space battleship was in orbit above the planet. Down on the planet's surface, a force of robot soldiers were attacking the planet's native population, orange-skinned, hairless beings attired in uniforms and wielding blaster weapons. The robots were firing blasters from their hands and exerting superhuman strength to overwhelm the Vetorian soldiers. All the robot soldiers looked exactly the same, metallic red with red optical sensors. There was another robot who descended from the clouds, riding a beam of light from the space battleship. That robot was humanoid as well, but he had a distinctive appearance compared to the other robots, being silver-toned. He had both hands clasped behind his back as a digital readout registered in his field of vision.

"Vetorian opposition down to 30 percent," the lead robot remarked, observing the battle below him as he descended toward the ground. "If the current state of affairs continues, the opposition will be reduced to 0 percent within two hours. If I join my Morobots in battle, we can shave an hour off that time.

"Sensors indicate a lingering ion trail from an Ardorian military ship. I will investigate this anomaly once we have conquered Vetoria. If an Ardorian has managed to survive the war, we will seek him out and destroy him. There will be no need to transmit a report. This matter will be taken care of. Continue forward and eliminate all resistance. Vetoria will fall before the forces of Moroborg."

A Vetorian soldier shot Moroborg with his blaster weapon, but the attack was ineffective against the mechanical menace. Moroborg cast his gaze upon the Vetorian who had shot him as digital information continued to register in his field of vision. The Vetorian soldier was shocked and dismayed by the failure of his attack.

"Data analysis indicates your weaponry to be ineffectual," Moroborg stated flatly. "Your technology is utterly inferior to mine."

Moroborg extended his hand toward the soldier, and he discharged a blaster bolt from the palm of his hand into the soldier's chest. The blaster bolt pierced through the armor of the chest plate of the soldier and exploded out of the back of the soldier, splattering blood from the wound. The soldier's eyes rolled back in his head as he collapsed to the ground and lay motionless where he fell.

"Now that I have joined the fray, Vetoria will fall within the hour," Moroborg decreed. "Eradicate all soldiers. Leave only civilians and the ruling class intact. Target any attacker with lethal response. Once inside their capital, we will assimilate all data concerning the Vetorians and the planet. We will then use said data to gain control of the masses and lay claim to the planet's resources."

Moroborg began flying along with thrusters in the heels of his feet, blasting Vetorian soldiers with powerful blaster bolts that sent them flying from the impact. The Morobots continued their domination of the soldiers as well, rebolstered by Moroborg's introduction into the battle. Moroborg used the blaster bolts from one hand while simultaneously employing his super strength with his other arm to execute soldiers. Moroborg moved to the front of the clash, leading the Morobots in battle personally.

Moroborg and his forces tore through the ranks of the soldiers. Some Morobots sustained damage from the battle, and some were disabled by the attacks of the soldiers, but others continued the clash. Moroborg received no damage from any of the attacks of the soldiers, despite drawing most of their fire. Moroborg displayed more superior strength and durability than the Morobots, and he appeared to be the only one capable of language. Otherwise, the Morobots were very similar in design and function to their master. The forces of Moroborg battled their way into the capitol building of the Vetorians, continuing to exterminate any who dared to try to fight them.

Moroborg fought his way to the main computer room of the building, blasting down the reinforced metal door. He made his way to the main console, and a cable extended out from his palm into the computer, data readouts still registering in his optic sensors. He began the process of downloading all data from their computers into himself. In a last-ditch effort to stop him, some of the soldiers tossed explosive devices into the computer room with Moroborg, and there was a massive explosion that resulted in a massive fire in the computer room.

All hope left the soldiers when they saw the silver-toned metallic body walking through the wall of flames unharmed, his optical sensors still registering readouts.

"Your last-ditch effort to stop me was a total failure," Moroborg stated the obvious, intimidating the soldiers. "I have completed the download of all data in your systems, assimilating it into my memory banks. I will now utilize this data to place you all under my dominant control. Your world will be lost to you in another fifty minutes. You, however, will not live to see it."

Moroborg stepped forward quickly and grabbed one soldier by the throat with one hand, choking him slowly. Moroborg then extended his other hand and sent another soldier flying through the air with a blaster bolt from that hand. Moroborg finally snapped the neck of the soldier he was choking, an almost effortless feat for him. While his Morobots found the soldiers to be a bit of trouble, Moroborg was impervious to their every attack and capable of easily dispatching his foes.

"I will find another terminal and download a control program into their remaining systems, thereby taking control of their technology," Moroborg declared. "Once such control is established, I will see all things perceptible to all sensors on the planet, and I will be able to direct the planet's technological weaponry to turn on its creators. I will subdue them with their own technology, their own weapons."

"Do you hear that, men?" a soldier asked rhetorically of his teammates. "We have to keep him from reaching another computer terminal at all costs! Employ any and all defenses available to stop him!"

"You can try," Moroborg suggested, brimming with overconfidence. "I must advise you, however, that I am substantially more advanced technologically than you are. My design makes me the ultimate living computer. I can process data at speeds faster than any other computer in the universe. I am programmed to assimilate data and conquer all. You will be no different than any I have encountered before. Your data has been assimilated into my memory banks, and you will be conquered in forty-five minutes."

Moroborg extended both hands simultaneously, discharging blaster bolts from both hands in unison. With a steady barrage of dual blaster bolts, Moroborg decimated his opposition. He then flew up through the floors of the building, smashing his way to the penthouse suite. Once there, he located another computer console in the chamber of the ruling class of that society. The room was surrounded by several venerable Vetorians in robes, those who ruled over their people. They were not soldiers; therefore they were neither armed nor armored.

"Activate defensive countermeasures now!" one of the Vetorian nobles cried out.

A protective field of energy appeared between Moroborg and the nobles. Also, heavy blasters emerged from the walls and ceiling, firing on Moroborg in rapid-fire fashion. Moroborg was jostled a bit from the impact, but he was unharmed by those attacks. Moroborg proceeded to the computer console and accessed it by that extending cable from his palm. A moment later, the heavy blasters that were firing upon him shut down. Then, the force field protecting the nobles shut down.

"He's overridden our control of the interior defenses!" one of the nobles exclaimed. "It's only a matter of time before he gains control of all our technology! We have to stop him... before it's too late!"

"It is already too late, inferior carbon-based life forms," Moroborg informed them. "The moment I connected with your computer console, I initiated program overrides of all of your technology. In the time it would take you to think about it, I have accomplished it. My control is established at the speed of thought, and I can process information over a thousand times faster than your pitiful protein brains.

"If the notion struck me, I could launch all of your missiles simultaneously upon whatever coordinates I choose on this planet. I could utterly destroy every living being on this planet with coordinated missile strikes followed by a systematic seek-and-destroy operation by my Morobots. My Morobots already have orders to exterminate all combatants on your planet. If you had control of your missiles, you might have stood a chance to defeat me, but, now that your most powerful weapons are under my control, you are incapable of threatening me.

"All Vetorian resistance will cease in forty-two minutes. After that, the rest of you will be under my control. Hope is nonexistent. I still have an army of Morobots on board my ship, which is orbiting your planet. Should I choose, I could call them down to this planet. Also, you are in no position to stop me. All of your defensive measures are turned off, and I control your missiles. It is highly illogical to resist any further. The outcome will not be averted by your best efforts."

"He can't be right!" one of the nobles proclaimed.

"But I am, and there is nothing you can do about it," Moroborg replied. "As a matter of fact, I deciphered the encrypted files protecting the locations of your various military bases, and I have targeted them all with missiles from your own arsenal. I calculate that tactic will shave off another twenty-five minutes from my schedule. In less than sixteen minutes, all resistance on this planet will be neutralized, and I can divert my attention to the pursuit of the Ardorian survivor whose ship's lingering ion trail I have detected."

Moroborg retracted his cable back into his hand, severing the physical connection he had with the computer console.

"My presence is no longer required here to complete this mission," Moroborg said. "I have now established long-range control of your technology. I can remotely control your weapons systems from interstellar distances. I will leave behind a contingent of my Morobots to finish the job while I pursue the Ardorian survivor. Your defeat is imminent. Victory is mine."

With that said, Moroborg flew up through the roof of the building, leaving the nobles to contemplate their fate. Moroborg flew straight up to his ship, boarding it. A moment later, the ship began flying away from the planet. Meanwhile, the missiles began descending into the atmosphere, streaking directly toward those military bases. The soldiers at those military bases were shocked and horrified to see the missiles descending upon them.

Chapter 11

Antarctica

Centurion was in a high-tech structure, sitting in a chair in front of a computer console and monitor. He studied the data flow at super speed, analyzing the computer's digital computations on the monitor.

"It seems you're faring much better than the humans who were affected by the unusual radiation of the meteor," the computer informed him. "They've all slipped into comas since falling ill."

"And there's nothing I can do," Centurion lamented.

"Their vitals are stable thus far. They're just in comas," the computer reported. "It appears your physiology is fighting off the radiation's effects. That's what has been causing your bouts of dizziness. As your body fights off the effects of the radiation poisoning, you are weakened somewhat as a result."

"How much longer before I'm back to normal?" Centurion asked.

"Insufficient data to calculate. Conclusion unknown," the computer answered. "Fortunately, everything seems calm at the moment."

"But for how long?" Centurion inquired rhetorically.

"As I said. Insufficient data to calculate. Conclusion unknown," the computer reiterated in response.

"I was being rhetorical," Centurion stated.

"Rhetorical. Asking a question without actually requiring an answer," the computer responded in its logical manner. "I'll work on recognizing rhetorical inquiries."

"I've never been affected by radiation before," Centurion muttered. "This is a strange scenario. Whatever energy was emanating from the meteor was highly irregular to say the least. I've encountered all kinds of radiation before, and my invulnerability protected me from those effects. This energy form somehow bypassed my invulnerability to afflict me. If I'm reading this right, it's affecting me on a cellular level."

"Correct," the computer chimed in. "The radiation effect is attacking you on a cellular level, as if it's trying to rewrite your DNA to some degree."

"That's odd," Centurion remarked as he pondered the notion.

"Very odd," the computer concurred. "Radiation typically breaks down a victim's biochemical physiology, producing a cancer of some sort, but this radiation appears to be attempting to alter your genetic structure by rewriting your DNA code. Some might regard this as an evolutionary transformation, but this transformation requires a catalyst."

"So, it's trying to alter me," Centurion surmised. "Then that's what it's doing to those humans who were affected. It's attempting to rewrite their DNA sequence to alter them at a cellular level. It's changing them from within."

"Correct," the computer confirmed his suspicions. "Whether or not such mutations will be of a benign nature is currently unknown; however, something within you is interfering with the mutagenic effects of the radiation poisoning. Your antibody count is extremely high, which indicates your body is fighting to reject the changes. It is unknown whether or not your body will succeed in rejecting the mutagenic process."

"Perhaps I hold the answer to the infection within my bloodstream," Centurion suggested. "If that's the case, I could synthesize a cure with a sample of my blood and hopefully save those humans who were infected."

"The likelihood of success is inconclusive at this point," the computer informed him. "In theory, it could work, but, in theory, it could also actually exacerbate their situation."

"Then we're back to square one," Centurion muttered in dismay.

"I'm afraid so," the computer replied.

"Continue to analyze the process with the genetic sample we've procured from my body," Centurion instructed the computer. "If there's a chance of generating an inoculation for the humans from my genetic response to the infection, I want to try it."

"Yes, sir," the computer responded.

"Also, keep me updated on any events I might need to respond to," Centurion added. "Just because I'm not at 100 percent doesn't mean I'm going to sit idly by while some event threatens innocent lives."

"Yes, sir," the computer acknowledged the request.

Chapter 12

The following day

Covenant City, Nevada

The scene was set for a press conference in the Covenant City park. Senator Atlas's security bots were positioned around the senator to shield him from danger. Ms. Watson stood a short distance behind him on stage, Mr. Williams standing next to her. Senator Atlas stood at the podium, looking out at the crowd of people in attendance. There were representatives of the media in attendance, including Claire Jackson and Dave Pierce. There were soldiers from General Hawkins's entourage stationed around the event as well, and General Hawkins was present to bear witness to the press conference.

"Ladies and gentlemen of the press, esteemed members of our armed forces, good citizens of Covenant City, thank you for joining me here today to discuss our future," Senator Atlas said. "Let me begin by saying we owe our citizenry protection from threats, be they terrorists or otherwise. We owe the populace the conviction and the vision to do what is right to protect them. We owe the people justice.

"Just a few short days ago, we were introduced to a visitor from the stars, an alien soldier with unbelievable powers. I have decided to refer to anyone with superhuman abilities as a supra, for simplicity's sake. This extraterrestrial supra has been quite active in my home city as of late. He's rescued you from a tornado, an apartment building fire, a disabled passenger plane that was about to crash into the city, a carload of hoodlums pumped up on illegal drugs and armed with firearms who were driving recklessly through the streets of the city, and myriad other things. For his timely assistance in these matters, we owe him thanks.

"Unfortunately, we can't be sure of his ulterior motives, his true intentions. For all we know, he might be an advance scout for an invasion force. We just don't know for sure. So, sure, he's done many good deeds since his arrival, including diverting that meteor over our nation just a few days ago, but what do we really know about him? What if he proves far less benign than we may wish to believe? What if he was to turn those amazing powers of his against us? What then? Well, ladies and gentlemen, I've come up with a few ideas to protect us from that possibility.

"First of all, I propose the creation of an agency whose sole purpose is to assess threats from superhuman beings and determine the threat level. I am naming this agency the SAC, or Supra Affairs Commission. They will be represented by some of the brightest military and scientific minds in the country. They will tirelessly analyze any potential threat to our safety from any being with superhuman abilities and gather information on any such beings who take up residence on our planet.

"Secondly, I am proposing the creation of a specialized police force to keep potential superhuman threats in line. If any being of great power decides to run amok in our cities and neighborhoods, it will be the mission of this police agency to subdue and capture the perpetrator. I have dubbed this task force the SPF, or Supra Police Force. Their ranks will be filled by some of the top military people and law enforcement officers we can find. Also, I've decided that Tech Labs should be the outfitters of these operatives. Tech Labs can do an admirable job of supplying the SPF with gear and tech to do their jobs.

"Thirdly, I am proposing the construction of a prison facility in which we can incarcerate beings no normal prison can hope to contain. I am dubbing this prison facility the SIF, or Supra Incarceration Facility. We will be tapping some of the most brilliant minds on the planet to equip and construct the facility with technology designed to counter any superhuman ability imaginable. If supras decide to threaten the people of this country, they will find themselves in a formidable holding facility for the duration of their sentence. They might think twice about terrorist or criminal actions after a stay at the SIF.

"As you may suspect, these proposals will cost money to implement, which is why I'm prepared to make a substantial donation to the process out of my own pockets. Perhaps we could redirect some funds already in circulation from other programs of a similar nature. Perhaps we could divert some defense spending temporarily into these programs, at least until we have them up and running. We might find some money elsewhere to supplement this project's financing. Of course, we might still have to ultimately increase spending in order to fund this vision. Despite this unpopular scenario, I am of the firm belief that we will need these things for our future safety.

"Imagine, if you will, Centurion turning on us. He possesses super strength, super speed, the power of flight, super senses, and what can best be described as invulnerability, according to his own words. He also can project heat beams from his eyes and powerful gusts of wind from his mouth. Those are just the abilities we know about. What if he turns those powers on us? How would we protect ourselves from him? We have soldiers, and they are a fine lot indeed, but, even well equipped for traditional warfare, could they actually protect us from the likes of Centurion? We have excellent men and women serving in law enforcement, but what can they do when the criminal in question can lift fully loaded passenger planes, fire laser beams from his eyes, and survive the harsh conditions of outer space without harm? What price do you put on peace of mind?

"Also, a number of human beings all over the world have fallen into comas in the aftermath of Centurion diverting that meteor over the continental United States off its collision course with Earth. The meteor would've hit our planet and possibly killed millions, even billions, but he managed to push it off course so that it missed our planet. However, we have reports of an unknown radiation having bathed the entire planet from this near miss. We've never encountered a situation like this one, so we don't know what it means to us yet. These unfortunate victims of circumstance could simply wake up tomorrow and ask for pizza, or things could get much worse for them. They could die in those comas. They could also be comatose for decades. Many of them have the best medical care watching over them, but, as we understand it, it's a waiting game at this point. Either they wake up or they don't. All we can do is wait and see.

"Our hearts go out to these people and their families. We hope they have a speedy and full recovery and awake to rejoin their loved ones in this game of life. We're grateful that the earth was spared a potential extinction-level event. The human race may yet survive for millennia more to come in the wake of this averted event. Of course, we don't know if there will be any further complications from the radiation bath our planet received from that meteor. For all we know, we could all now die of cancer, and Centurion would inherit the earth, provided he survives the radiation bath.

"As ever, we live in an uncertain world. There is much to fear out there—terrorists, natural disasters, collapsing money markets, and the like. We worry that crazed dictators and terrorists will acquire nuclear weapons. We fear another financial collapse like we experienced in 2008. We have gangs and criminals that threaten the safety of our populace. Drugs are still a threat to our people, especially our children. People are killing people for little or nothing, sometimes rationalized by religious zealotry. Crime has been on a steady rise over the last few decades. Sometimes it's difficult to hold on to hope.

"As a nation, we struggle with it all. As a planet, we struggle with it all. Once upon a time, we could sleep with our doors unlocked. Now, we don't dare do such a thing. Now, we have people kicking open doors to homes, invading those homes, and victimizing the families inside those homes. Once upon a time, people worked for everything they had. Nowadays, some people just steal it and call it theirs. We live in very different times, ladies and gentlemen. Now, in the twenty-first century, we face things we never have before."

Suddenly, a horde of Morobots descended upon the city.

"What in the world?!?" Senator Atlas exclaimed in shock.

People started running in all directions, fleeing from the invading robots. Senator Atlas's security bots saw to his escape, along with Ms. Watson and Mr. Williams. The soldiers and police officers stepped up to defend the civilians from the Morobots. As that was going on, Senator Atlas's entourage made it back to his limo.

"Get me to Atlascorp pronto, Mr. Williams!" Senator Atlas instructed his employee.

"You're not—" Mr. Williams began to respond.

"Don't argue with me, man! Just do as you're told!" Senator Atlas scolded Mr. Williams as they began piling into the limo.

Meanwhile, the soldiers and policemen found themselves helpless against the Morobots, and they began falling back in the face of their overwhelming foes. Claire and Dave took cover and began covering the story as it broke.

Chapter 13

Antarctica

Centurion was sitting in front of that computer console and monitor again, watching the data stream on the screen with his super speed. Suddenly, the computer interrupted that with an urgent message.

"Sir, Covenant City is under attack from an extraterrestrial invasion," the computer advised the hero. "The ship just dropped out of hyperspace in orbit around the earth, and robots descended upon Covenant City. Sir, the ship is of Morovian design."

Without a word, Centurion bolted from the structure at super speed, flying from Antarctica toward North America. His visage was contorted with concern and a hint of exertion as he flew along, breaking the sound barrier in an instant.

"I'm still suffering from the debilitating effects of the radiation poisoning," Centurion reported. "I'm unable to attain top speed, so it's going to take me a little time to get there."

"Understood, sir," the computer acknowledged.

Centurion pushed himself for more speed, frantically trying to reach Covenant City in time. He zipped over the water as he traversed the distance. There was a great sense of urgency about him as he flew over South America, closing on Mexico. Sometime later, he was passing over the border between Mexico and the United States. Minutes after that, he arrived in Covenant City to see the invasion in process. Centurion flew toward the Morobots, a determined look upon his face.

Suddenly, he was shot out of the sky by a blaster bolt. He crashed to the pavement below, sliding through the pavement and into the side of a building. Centurion struggled to get to his feet, a hand to his head as the dizziness was affecting him again. He placed his other hand on the side of that building to steady himself. At that point, he was hit three times in succession in the chest and upper torso by blaster bolts, driving him backward a few steps and dropping him to one knee.

Centurion trained his vision on a group of Morobots advancing on his position. Twin beams of heat shot out of his eyes and sliced through those Morobots, dropping them where they stood. Centurion then rose to full height, fighting against the dizziness. A Morobot closed on him and rocked him with a punch to the face. Another Morobot clipped him with a passing punch in flight, staggering Centurion backward. Centurion exhaled a gust of super breath to blow those two Morobots away from him a great distance.

The police and the military began a strategic withdrawal, finding their weapons useless against the armored hides of the Morobots. Centurion managed a triple strike, targeting three Morobots at super speed, and those attacks knocked those three Morobots down, but Centurion became dizzy again, struggling to retain his balance. A trio of Morobots targeted Centurion with their blaster bolts, hitting him in the chest simultaneously and knocking him down. Centurion used his eyebeams to slice through those three Morobots, cutting each one in half.

Centurion got back to his feet in a daze. A Morobot landed right in front of Centurion and rocked him with a series of punches to the face. Centurion finally managed to catch the Morobot's fist in his hand, interrupting its onslaught. Before Centurion could take advantage of that opportunity, another Morobot crashed into him like a missile, driving him backward as his feet dug trails through the ground in the park and causing him to release his grip on that one Morobot's fist. The Morobot whose fist was freed from Centurion's grasp fired a blaster bolt from its hand into Centurion's chest, rocking him backward. The Morobot who had speared Centurion from across the park fired a blaster bolt into Centurion as well, knocking him down on the ground again.

Centurion sliced the closer Morobot in half with his eyebeams and then got back to his feet, a little addled. The other Morobot flew at Centurion in an attempt to spear him. Centurion greeted that Morobot with an uppercut, decapitating the robot and sending its head flying into the sky. From there Centurion flew up into the sky, blasting a few Morobots along the way with his eyebeams, disabling them as he streaked upwards. Centurion was then hit from multiple directions by blaster bolts from Morobots, rocking him. All of a sudden, a more potent blaster bolt from the spaceship above sent him crashing through some trucks below.

Chapter 14

Back at Atlascorp, Senator Atlas had donned a bulky suit of high-tech battle armor. Dr. Cross, Mr. Williams, and Ms. Watson were standing in the room with him.

"So, how does it feel?" Dr. Cross asked Senator Atlas.

"It feels good," Senator Atlas answered happily. "I must commend you, Dr. Cross. This is quite a piece of work you've delivered."

"Sir, maybe you should let me into that armor suit," Mr. Williams volunteered.

"No, Mr. Williams. This is my time now," Senator Atlas replied. "I will take my place among heroes past. I have this one."

"Sir, what if things go badly?" Ms. Watson inquired in concern.

"My dear Ms. Watson, have more confidence in me," Senator Atlas implored her. "I will use this battle suit to single handedly thwart this alien invasion, and I will bring down that spaceship above our fair city. Now, Dr. Cross, open the door and let me put this battle suit to the test."

"As you wish, sir," Dr. Cross responded as he pressed a button on a computer console, causing a portion of the wall to open up.

Senator Atlas flew out of the building via the thrusters in his battle suit's boots. He headed straight toward the spaceship in orbit over the earth. He fired his battle suit's blasters from the palms of the armor's hands, causing some damage to the spaceship. In response, Moroborg descended from the belly of the ship.

"What's this? A doorman?" Senator Atlas joked as he hovered below the spaceship in preparation to do battle with Moroborg.

"I am Moroborg," Moroborg introduced himself.

"I am Senator Alexander Aaron Atlas," Senator Atlas identified himself. "Are you in charge of this invasion force?"

"I am," Moroborg admitted without fear.

"Then you're the one I want," Senator Atlas replied.

"This is a mistake that will cost you dearly," Moroborg advised him.

"We'll just have to see about that," Senator Atlas responded, his confidence rising as he extended the palm of his hand toward Moroborg.

Senator Atlas fired his blasters again, hitting Moroborg flush with them, but they had seemingly no effect upon Moroborg. Senator Atlas was a bit concerned by that outcome.

"Your attack was insufficient to do damage," Moroborg informed him.

"That's not good," Senator Atlas lamented in dismay.

"Allow me to show you how it's done," Moroborg suggested as he pointed the open palm of his hand toward Senator Atlas.

"Oh crap!" Senator Atlas muttered under his breath.

Moroborg discharged a powerful blaster bolt into the armored Senator Atlas, doing substantial damage to the senator's battle suit. Senator Atlas plummeted from the sky in the aftermath of that explosive attack, smoldering in his descent. After falling a great distance, Senator Atlas regained control with his boot thrusters, the damaged portion of his armor sparking and smoking. Moroborg descended toward his foe, using his boot thrusters to initiate a controlled fall. Senator Atlas fired his blasters into Moroborg, failing to do damage to the high-tech robot. As Moroborg closed on Senator Atlas, Senator Atlas turned Moroborg's head with a mighty punch. Senator Atlas threw another punch at Moroborg, but Moroborg caught Senator Atlas's armored fist in his hand, stopping the attack.

"Your strength is insufficient to do damage," Moroborg advised him.

Moroborg spun Senator Atlas around and flung him to the ground. Moroborg then alighted upon the ground and began striding forward toward his prey. Senator Atlas struggled to get back to his feet, dazed from the crash. As Senator Atlas stood up, Moroborg rocked him with a punch to the face plate. Moroborg doubled Senator Atlas over with a punch to the midsection. Moroborg then knocked Senator Atlas down the street and into a car with a mighty back fist strike, flipping the car through the air in the process. Senator Atlas slowly pried himself from the wreckage, ending up on one knee.

"Dr. Cross, your battle suit is not faring so well," Senator Atlas informed the chief inventor of Atlascorp over the comm system.

"Sir, the opposition must be extraordinary for the battle suit to be found lacking," Dr. Cross proclaimed in disbelief.

"I'm battling the leader of the invasion, a robotic being who calls himself Moroborg," Senator Atlas explained. "I can't put a dent in his armor, but he's damaged my armor."

"Perhaps a strategic withdrawal would be in order," Dr. Cross suggested.

"I might not have that option," Senator Atlas remarked as he looked over to see Moroborg walking toward him.

"If you wish to flee, feel free to do so," Moroborg declared as he stopped advancing. "You're no threat to me. This battle is meaningless."

"You're damaged," Senator Atlas said as he rose to his feet. "You must really be damaged if you're willing to let me get away. I'll bet you're bluffing."

"I do not bluff," Moroborg replied adamantly.

"Oh, you're good," Senator Atlas chuckled. "I may not have pierced your armor, but I must've rattled you inside that metallic shell of yours. If I keep fighting, I might just shut you down. That prospect must scare you."

"I am Moroborg, and I have no fear," Moroborg declared.

"Well, let's just find out, okay?" Senator Atlas chuckled.

Senator Atlas peppered Moroborg with blaster bolts, but the robot just stood there looking at the armor-clad politician. Moroborg then began walking forward. Senator Atlas began to worry about his situation once again. Moroborg stopped right in front of Senator Atlas, standing up to the blaster bolt barrage. Moroborg then grabbed Senator Atlas's outstretched hand and squeezed, damaging the gauntlet of the armor and crippling the blaster effect in that gauntlet.

"Perhaps you should've listened to me after all," Moroborg suggested with a hint of sarcasm in his robotic retort.

"Well, I'm not one to simply roll over just because someone tells me to, but I'll be happy to make an exception in this instance," Senator Atlas offered his surrender.

"You are an annoying man, Senator Alexander Aaron Atlas," Moroborg insulted Senator Atlas before sending him crashing through a storefront window with a punch, doing even more damage to his battle suit.

"I've never been called that before," Senator Atlas gasped as he struggled to stand up in the storefront, crawling from underneath fallen mannequins and articles of clothing.

"Do yourself a favor and stay down," Moroborg advised Senator Atlas.

With that said, Moroborg knocked Senator Atlas further into the store with a blaster bolt to the chest plate of his battle suit. Senator Atlas gasped in pain and then lay limp and motionless on the floor, releasing a moan of agony as he succumbed to the temptation to do as he was advised and stay down. Moroborg then looked toward the park.

"The Ardorian appears to have been weakened by something unknown," Moroborg commented. "I should step in and put him down myself."

Chapter 15

Centurion stood in the middle of the park, his breathing labored. All around him lay the scraps of the Morobots, the remains of the invading army. He looked around to make sure all of them were down, and then his gaze met that the military and police. They smiled joyously. Suddenly, a powerful blaster bolt slammed into Centurion's back and sent him sliding in the dirt across the park. Centurion raised his upper torso up off the ground with his arms and shook his head. An instant later, a mechanical hand reached down and grabbed Centurion by the hair of his head. Moroborg lifted Centurion to his feet by his hair and examined him.

"You are identified as Captain Conlan Lar of the Ardorian Centurions," Moroborg identified the hero.

"Well, here they just call me Centurion," Centurion informed him.

"So I've heard," Moroborg replied. "I have intercepted transmissions from planet side and retro-scanned prior transmissions from the last few days. I am well aware what the people of this pathetic planet call you. Today, you will die, and then the entire planet."

With that said, Moroborg tossed Centurion across the park and into a tree. Centurion bounced off the tree and then bounced off the ground. Moroborg began striding forward as Centurion struggled to get to his feet.

"I was programmed to expect more from an Ardorian Centurion," Moroborg retorted with a hint of disdain in his voice as he approached Centurion.

"Sorry to disappoint you, but I've been feeling a bit under the weather lately," Centurion replied just before blasting Moroborg with his eyebeams.

Moroborg stumbled backward a couple of steps, but his armor wasn't damaged by the attack. Centurion looked dismayed by that result. Moroborg resumed his march toward Centurion, undeterred in his intent. Moroborg doubled Centurion over with a punch to the midsection, and then he rocked Centurion backward with an uppercut to the face. Moroborg staggered Centurion backward with a backhand swipe across the face, casually advancing on him to continue the clash.

"Your death will conclude your misbegotten race, Conlan," Moroborg said as he rocked Centurion with yet another punch to the face. "At long last, we shall see the end of the Ardorians in our universe."

Centurion threw a punch at Moroborg, but the robot blocked the attack with his forearm. Moroborg grabbed Centurion by the throat with his other hand. The veins in Centurion's head bulged as the robotic villain squeezed the Ardorian's neck.

"I know you don't need to breathe," Moroborg commented. "But I can still commit physical harm via brute force."

Moroborg forced Centurion to one knee with his chokehold. Centurion grabbed Moroborg's hand with both hands, managing to pry the robot's hand from around his neck. Moroborg then doubled Centurion over with a punch to the midsection. Next, Moroborg grabbed Centurion by the back of his attire and tossed him through a vending truck in the park, bouncing him off a tree on the other side of that truck.

Moroborg walked over to the damaged vending truck and ripped it in half with his brute strength, clearing a direct path to the downed hero. Centurion stood up again in a daze. Moroborg began pummeling him with punches to the face, turning his head with each punch and cracking the tree behind him as well. In seconds, Moroborg knocked Centurion through the tree with a punch, and the tree fell to the side of Moroborg.

Centurion struggled to get to his feet again, and Moroborg staggered Centurion with another punch to the face. Moroborg grabbed Centurion by the hair of the head and pounded him in the midsection with the other hand repeatedly. Moroborg then ripped a punch to the head of Centurion, staggering the hero backward as he released his grasp of the Ardorian's hair. An instant later, a rocket slammed into Moroborg from behind, exploding. Centurion stumbled backward and dropped to one knee, shielding his face from the explosion with his arm. A soldier with a rocket launcher watched from across the park.

When the smoke cleared, Moroborg was unharmed by the attack. Moroborg turned toward the soldier with the rocket launcher, and the terrified soldier quickly began trying to reload the rocket launcher for another shot.

"That is quite the armament," Moroborg commended him halfheartedly. "Now that you have my attention, you will be sorry."

Moroborg extended his hand toward the soldier loading the rocket launcher, preparing to fire his blaster bolt at him. There was a blur of motion as Moroborg fired a blaster bolt at the soldier. There was an explosion where the blaster bolt hit. When the smoke cleared, Centurion stood between the unharmed soldier and his metallic foe, breathing heavily with a determined look in his eyes. Moroborg tilted his head, a gesture indicating his confusion.

"You appear to be feeling much better now," Moroborg remarked.

"Not good news for you," Centurion replied as he seared a hole in Moroborg's armored hide with his eyebeams.

Moroborg looked down at the hole in his chest plate and then back at Centurion. Centurion smiled. Centurion then flew forward at great speed and slammed into Moroborg, flying straight up into the sky with him a moment later. In the sky, the two of them began exchanging punches as they raced ever higher. Moments later, they were in space, high above the earth, and Centurion knocked Moroborg backward toward his spaceship with a mighty punch to the chest, denting the chest plate of the robot's armored hide. Moroborg looked at the dent in his chest, and then he looked back at Centurion.

Centurion grimaced in rage as he flew at Moroborg at super speed. Centurion slammed into Moroborg again, driving completely through the huge spaceship and out the other side with Moroborg. Moroborg drifted away from the spaceship, his red optical sensors flickering. Centurion directed his attention to the spaceship and disabled its engines with his eyebeams, leaving it crippled in space. Centurion then destroyed all external armaments of the spaceship with his eyebeams.

Moroborg's optic sensors flickered back on, and he fired a blaster beam at Centurion. Centurion sought to counter that with his eyebeams, but Moroborg's blaster beam began slowly pushing Centurion's eyebeams back toward him. Centurion strained his eyebeams to push back against Moroborg's blaster beam, but the blaster beam kept pushing toward him. Moroborg's blaster beam drove back into Centurion, knocking him from orbit and back into the earth's atmosphere. The massive ship's orbit began deteriorating as it drifted into the gravitational pull of the planet. Moroborg pursued Centurion back into the earth's atmosphere to resume the battle.

"It can't be," Moroborg said in dismay. "You've actually damaged my body."

"You said it yourself. I feel much better now," Centurion taunted him. "For the first time in the last couple of days, I feel like myself again."

"Sir, your body has fully rejected the radiation poisoning from the meteor," Centurion's computer reported to him in his comm link.

"That's what I thought," Centurion replied with a smile on his face.

"You've established a base here on this planet," Moroborg surmised. "You're in communication with your base computer as we speak, aren't you?"

"I am, and I just received a clean diagnosis," Centurion admitted.

"Let me tap into your comm link, Conlan," Moroborg implored the hero in taunting fashion as he prepared to renew his attack.

"You'll have to get much closer to do that," Centurion advised him.

"Then I shall," Moroborg replied as he flew toward Centurion.

Centurion caught Moroborg's wrists in his hands, restraining him. The extension devices reached out from Moroborg's hands, but he quite couldn't reach Centurion's head with them. Centurion sliced off Moroborg's hands with his eyebeams, disabling the extension devices as well.

"You've taken my hands," Moroborg muttered.

"And with them, your blasters too," Centurion reminded him. "Now, not only are you not tapping into my comm link, but you won't be using those annoying blaster attacks anymore. Now it's just a hand-to-hand fight, and there are no more of your minions to help you out of this."

"You have defeated all of my Morobots, but I cannot permit you to live," Moroborg decreed. "I will find a way to kill you."

Centurion drove his fist deep into the interior of Moroborg's chest cavity, and Moroborg's optical sensors began flickering once more. Centurion then slammed his fist into Moroborg's face, punching straight through his head. At that time, his optical sensors flickered off, and he went limp. Centurion pulled his hands out of Moroborg's anatomy and watched the robot fall toward the ground. Then, Centurion looked up to see the giant spaceship beginning to enter the earth's atmosphere. With a determined expression on his face, he flew up to meet the spaceship.

Centurion flew underneath the ship and began pushing upward, slowing the spaceship's descent a little. However, the ship kept falling toward the ground. Centurion strained harder and harder, pushing against the plummeting ship with all his might. The ship slowed gradually as it closed with the ground, and then Centurion cried out in exertion. With a renewed sense of urgency, Centurion stopped the spaceship's plunge and began flying it back out into space. Upon getting the spaceship out into space, he hurled it toward the sun in the weightlessness of space. Satisfied that the spaceship would be no more a menace to the earth, Centurion turned his gaze earthward, and then he headed back to the city.

Chapter 16

Covenant City, Nevada

Centurion stood on the roof of the *Covenant City Crier* building with Claire Jackson. She stood close to the middle of the rooftop, and he stood at the edge of the rooftop, staring down over the city. There was a serenity and calm in the air.

"So, how does it feel to be hailed as a champion of the planet?" Claire asked.

"I'm just glad there's still a planet," Centurion answered. "I'm not here for fame and glory. I'm here to stand up for those who can't stand up for themselves."

"You were looking a little sickly back there for a while," Claire remarked.

"You remember that meteor I diverted?" Centurion inquired.

"Yeah. What was it, four days ago?" Claire replied.

"It bathed the entire Earth in some strange radiation that even I wasn't immune to," Centurion informed her. "I was battling these odd bouts of dizziness for the past couple of days until my body fought off the effects of its own accord."

"All those other people who were affected are still in comas," Claire said.

"I just wish I'd known about the meteor before it got that close to Earth," Centurion lamented, a somber visage upon him. "It was moving pretty fast. Who knows what that radiation will do to those people?"

"Hopefully, they'll pull through just like you did," Claire suggested.

"I'm Ardorian. I'm made of sterner stuff than humans," Centurion reminded her. "I share your prayer for a miracle, but I do have my concerns."

"Yeah, we humans aren't able to lift giant spaceships and hurl them out into space or bounce bullets off our chests, but not all of us are suffering from radiation poisoning," Claire responded. "Who knows? Maybe some scientist might be able to make a serum from those of us who have thus far been immune to the radiation's effects."

"I'd like to share your optimism," Centurion stated with a brief smile. "I've faced a lot of doubt since I lost my family and my people. Sometimes hope is hard to grasp."

"That's why we grab hold so tightly," Claire advised him.

"It's why we cling so defiantly to it," Centurion added with a contented countenance. "Believe me, I'm hoping for the best, but I sometimes fear for the worst. I guess lately I've been so busy fighting an uphill battle to protect the innocent that I've lost sight of the best in all of us because I get to see the worst of people in horrendous action. Sometimes I just have to step out of the mix to regain my perspective."

"I'm afraid we all do," Claire responded in empathy. "It's nice to know sometimes that, despite the fact you're so much more powerful than humans, you still share some of the same basic fears and hopes that we do."

"My upbringing wasn't really much different from yours," Centurion said with a smile as he turned around toward her. "We had morals and convictions, along with fears and hopes. We felt outrage over injustices. We hoped for a better tomorrow. I still do. I may have lost my family and my people, but I now have a new home where I'm more welcomed than I used to be. That feels good."

"You've earned it, so enjoy it," Claire insisted with a smile on her face. "You know, if not for you, a lot of people would probably have gotten killed. Because you cared, we're still around. Thank you."

"That's what friends are for, right?" Centurion asked rhetorically.

"So, what do you do for an encore?" Claire inquired.

"I don't know," Centurion said, glancing back over his shoulder at the city. "We'll just have to see what the future has in store."

"So... what was up with those robots?" Claire asked.

"I don't know, but their leader knew a lot about my people, and he even knew my name," Centurion answered. "I can't help feeling like there's something familiar about him. He even knew my rank. Their spacecraft was of Morovian design. That means that those robots were either built by the Morovians, or they commandeered a battleship from the Morovians at some point. The Morovians were the people who destroyed my planet."

"That's a little creepy," Claire remarked.

"Yes, it is," Centurion agreed. "Anyway, I see the military took custody of Moroborg's body after the fight, along with the scraps and remains of the Morobots."

"Yeah, that was awfully convenient of them," Claire chuckled.

"Fortunately, the spaceship they came in got a one-way ticket to the sun," Centurion declared. "I was worried that one of those robots might be able to transfer itself into the computers on that spaceship and simply build another body for itself."

"I really hadn't thought of that," Claire commented. "Can they do that?"

"There was a possibility," Centurion confessed. "I just didn't want to take that chance. I wouldn't want Moroborg to threaten the earth again."

"We definitely don't want that," Claire concurred. "What do you think will happen with the military having custody of the robots' bodies?"

"I'm just hoping Moroborg doesn't come back online and transfer his programming into a military computer," Centurion replied.

"That would be very bad," Claire surmised.

"Very bad indeed," Centurion agreed.

Chapter 17

Senator Atlas lay in a hospital bed. Ms. Watson and Mr. Williams stood at his bedside. Senator Atlas was fuming as he lay in that bed.

"I can't believe it," Senator Atlas muttered in dismay. "Not only do I fail to stop Moroborg and his robot army, but Centurion comes along and saves the day in my stead. To make matters worse, I find myself here in the hospital."

"You're gonna be okay, sir," Mr. Williams assured him.

"Oh, I'll recover from the beating Moroborg dished out to me, but I still won't be okay," Senator Atlas decreed. "I failed to save my hometown from this invasion of robots, and then Centurion eclipsed my efforts by defeating the robot invaders single handedly. He'll be on the front page of every newspaper in the world, the main story of every television newscast on the planet, and I'll be lucky to get an honorable mention. Additionally, my battle suit was heavily damaged in the battle, and it may be a long time before it's ready to be put back in the field again."

"The important thing is you have no permanent injuries as a result of putting yourself in harm's way out there," Ms. Watson reminded him. "You can use your powers of persuasion to woo the people as you regale them with tales of your heroism."

"That was pretty hard core, boss," Mr. Williams commended him.

"Yes, it was," Senator Atlas chuckled. "Still, if I don't tell my story, it won't be told. That, my friends, is a travesty. The media should be fawning at my feet for the story of a lifetime. United States Senator challenges invaders in battle. How many other government personnel had the guts to get involved like I did? Even the military was helpless against Moroborg and his robot army. Even Centurion had his hands full with them.

"I think that battle suit should be retired. I need a new battle suit, an improved battle suit. I will have Dr. Cross begin work on it immediately. If my battle suit had been more powerful, maybe I could've defeated Moroborg. I was able to hit him with multiple attacks, but I couldn't manage to do damage to him. If the exoskeletal enhancement and the blasters had been more potent, maybe I could've won the battle myself. Then *I* would've earned the praise of the masses. Then *I* would've been the hero.

"Instead, I lie here in this hospital bed while that accursed alien freak gets all the glory. This is the most revolting day of my life. I can't believe such a day has come. I suffer a great indignity by being defeated at the hands of Moroborg, and then I suffer a great indignity when Centurion saves the day instead of me. Surely this day will haunt me for the rest of my life. I can't stand the thought that the whole world will be singing the praises of that stupid alien soldier while I get no recognition. How absurd is this?"

"Once you get back on your feet again, you'll get to tell your side of the story," Ms. Watson assured him. "Until then, we will sing your praises to the media, who will share your story of greatness with the rest of the world. When you're back on your feet, the media moguls will be begging to get an interview with you."

"Yes," Senator Atlas agreed. "They will be begging to hear the story from my own lips, and, when they do, they'll get the interview of a lifetime. I will not let this moment set me back. I will rise from the ashes like the phoenix of legend. This, combined with my proposals for agencies to deal with matters such as this, will further cement my senatorial legacy. It will also serve to help my future bid for the presidency."

"Looks like this is a win-win situation after all," Mr. Williams suggested.

"Indeed," Senator Atlas declared with a smile.

Chapter 18

Six days later

Washington, DC

General Hawkins sat in the room full of suited men again, prepared to give his report. Each had a file folder opened up in front of him.

"As you know, I recently made a trip to Covenant City to investigate this Centurion character, and I got to see his work in person," General Hawkins reported. "I interviewed Claire Jackson of the *Covenant City Crier*, and I met with representatives of Tech Labs and Atlascorp for further insight. Senator Atlas held a press conference in Covenant City in which he was outlining his plans for the future. It was during that press conference that an invasion force from space attacked the proceedings. I put my unit into action fighting against the robots from space, but we were outmatched by our foes. Senator Atlas employed a suit of powered armor to battle the robots' leader in single combat, but he was quickly crushed by that leader, who was called Moroborg. Everything looked bleak until Centurion arrived on the scene to intervene on our behalf.

"Initially, Centurion was having trouble with those robots and with Moroborg, too. Apparently, he was suffering from some sort of radiation poisoning from that meteor he deflected earlier this week. Toward the end of the fight, he seemed to fully recover from that radiation poisoning, and he promptly stomped a mudhole in that alien machine Moroborg and his minions. Upon Moroborg's defeat, his spaceship shut down and was drawn into Earth's gravity, and it began falling toward the planet's surface. Centurion managed to catch the spaceship, stop its descent, and fly it back out into space. According to our instruments, he hurled that spaceship toward the sun. He said he did that so that the none of the robots could transmit its consciousness, or program, back to the spaceship to later reform a body and return to attack us again.

"From what I witnessed, he acted selflessly in that effort to protect us and defeat the alien invaders. He could've allowed the alien robots to have their way with us. Also, he could've joined forces with the invaders in attacking us. Instead, he sided with us, and he endured substantial abuse in the process. He acted heroically on our behalf and without hesitation. It is my opinion that he is sincere in his representation of himself. I believe he is here to protect us from whatever threats may come our way. I believe he has our best interests at heart. He made certain all of us got out of this scrape alive, taking the full load of the battle upon himself while we evacuated the area. He saved a lot of people out there, both civilian and otherwise."

"You seriously expect us to take this assessment at face value?" one of the suited men challenged the notion.

"That is what you sent me in there for," General Hawkins responded. "As I recall, you wanted me to assess the situation, and that's what I've done. I can't help it if you don't like my assessment, but you're free to be wrong if you want to."

"Very well," another of the men stated. "We will take this assessment under advisement, and we will enter it into the record as such. Now, what news do we have on the people who were in comas in the wake of Centurion deflecting that meteor?"

"Some of them have awakened, and they now possess superpowers of their own," one of them answered. "However, not all of them are behaving like upstanding human beings. According to tests that have been performed over the duration of those people's comas, they have been altered on a cellular level. They are now what we've come to call supras, which is to say that they are people with super powers. Those who have not yet awakened from their comas are still undergoing radical transformations on the cellular level. It is just a matter of time before they awaken and we discover their abilities."

"It appears we will be implementing Senator Atlas's contingency plan after all," a suited man surmised. "Speaking of the senator, how is he?"

"He is in the hospital recovering from injuries he sustained in the effort to deter the invasion from space," another of the men replied. "He appears to be doing well."

"That's good," the man in charge said. "Let's set things in motion."

The man picked up a phone on the table next to him and dialed a number. He then held the receiver to his ear and waited as it rang, waiting for someone to answer.

"Project SPF is a go," the man said into the phone.

www.ingramcontent.com/pod-product-compliance
Lightning Source LLC
LaVergne TN
LVHW011850060526
838200LV00054B/4271